Every new generation of children is enthralled by the famous stories in our Well-Loved Tales series. Younger ones love to have the story read to them. Older children will enjoy the exciting stories in an easy-to-read text.

© LADYBIRD BOOKS LTD MCMLXXXIV
Loughborough, England
LADYBIRD BOOKS, INC.
Lewiston, Maine 04240 U.S.A.

Printed in England

The Firebird

retold by DOROTHY AITCHISON

illustrated by MARTIN AITCHISON

Ladybird Books

THE FIREBIRD

Many years ago in Russia, there lived a powerful king. A king in that country was called a Tsar. The gardens around the Tsar's palace had many beautiful trees and flowers, but his greatest treasure was a tree on which golden apples grew. The Tsar was very proud of this tree, and went to look at it every day.

Then one day, an apple was missing! The next day, another apple was missing! When a third apple disappeared, the Tsar grew angry. He ordered men to watch, but nobody could catch the thief.

The Tsar had three sons. The eldest was called
Peter, the second Vassily, and the youngest was
named Ivan. One day he called the young men to
his room.

"A robber is stealing my golden apples," said
the Tsar, "and I have decided that whoever can
catch this villain may have half my kingdom."

The eldest son stepped forward. "We will do
our best, Father," he said. "I will be first. I will
watch in the orchard tonight."

So Peter went to the garden to keep watch by the golden apple tree. He did his best to stay awake, but it was no good. In the morning he found that another apple had disappeared while he was asleep.

Peter had to tell his father that he had not caught the thief, and the Tsar told his second son to go to the orchard on the next night. Vassily had no better luck than Peter. Although he tried just as hard to stay awake, he too fell asleep. When daylight came, yet another apple had disappeared.

The Tsar was disappointed in his sons. When Ivan said he would watch over the tree on the third night, his father did not have much hope. "Go if you like," he said, "but I think you will fail, just as your brothers have."

Ivan took his place by the tree and decided that he would not sit down. He walked for many hours, and whenever he felt sleepy, he washed his eyes in the dew. At last he had his reward. Suddenly there was a flash of golden light, and a glittering bird with shining feathers flew up to the tree. Ivan watched as the creature began to peck with its jeweled beak at a golden apple. He crept silently toward the bird and grasped its tail. The bird broke free and fluttered away, but Ivan was left with a beautiful shining feather in his hand.

The next morning Ivan took the feather to his father, and the Tsar was very pleased. "It must have been the Firebird!" he said, when Ivan told him what had happened. Then the Tsar began to think that the Firebird would be an even greater treasure than his golden apples.

One day he sent for his sons. "I have decided that I must have the Firebird," he said. "Saddle your horses and go in search of it. Don't forget: if you succeed, you may have half my kingdom!"

Peter and Vassily set out at once, but the Tsar told Ivan that he was too young to go. This made Ivan very unhappy. He pleaded with his father, and reminded him that *he* had seen the Firebird already.

At last the Tsar agreed, and Ivan put on his armor and rode into the forest. He traveled for several days until he came to a large stone. He dismounted to read the message that was carved on it. The message said:

> "Go ahead and you will be hungry.
> Go left and you will die.
> Go right and you will lose your horse."

Ivan thought for a while and then decided to take the path to the right. He had been riding all day when suddenly a huge gray wolf darted from the bushes. The wolf pounced on Ivan, toppling him from his horse, which fled into the forest. "You read the message on the stone!" cried the wolf, and he bounded away.

Poor Ivan had to walk now.
He became very tired, and was sure that he would never find the Firebird.

At last he sat down to rest. Almost at once, the wolf appeared again. "I am sorry I frightened your horse away," he said, "but you saw the message on the stone. If you are so weary, tell me where you are going and I will carry you."

"I am looking for the Firebird who stole my father's golden apples," replied Ivan.

"Only I know where the Firebird lives. He belongs to a Tsar called Afron," said Gray Wolf.

"Climb on my back and I will take you."

As soon as Ivan had climbed on, the wolf ran swiftly through the forest. At last they came to a high stone wall.

"You will find the Firebird there," whispered Gray Wolf, "but take care. Whatever you do, you must *not* touch its cage."

Ivan climbed over the wall, and there indeed was the beautiful Firebird, in a golden cage. Forgetting all about Gray Wolf's warning, he seized the golden cage.

All at once bells began to ring, and guards ran up from every side.

"Stop, thief!" shouted the soldiers as Ivan turned to run.

They caught Ivan and brought him before Tsar Afron, who was very angry.

"Why do you come here and try to steal my property?" he roared.

Ivan was ashamed. "Sire, your Firebird stole my father's golden apples, and he told me to catch it," he said.

"Why didn't you ask me honestly, instead of trying to steal it?" asked the Tsar. "Perhaps I would have given it to you. Now I must tell

everybody that you are a thief." Then Tsar Afron saw how ashamed Ivan was. "I might forget what you have done if you will do something for me. In the next kingdom there is a horse with a golden mane. Bring it to me and

I will give you the Firebird." Ivan agreed eagerly, and the soldiers set him free. He hurried back to Gray Wolf, who was waiting outside. When he had heard all that had happened, Gray Wolf said, "I told you not to touch the cage! But come along, I will carry you to the next kingdom."

Swiftly the wolf carried Ivan through the forest until they came to the courtyard of a large castle. "Go quietly," whispered Gray Wolf. "The horse is in there. But no matter what, do *not* touch the bridle."

As Ivan tiptoed into the stable, he could hear the grooms talking next door. He found a splendid charger with a shining golden mane standing in a stall. Ivan wondered how he could quietly lead him out, when he saw a bridle hanging on the wall. Without thinking, he took it down and slipped it onto the horse.

Suddenly there was a great commotion, and Ivan was surrounded by angry servants.

"Our master will punish you," shouted the men. "Tsar Kusman never lets his prisoners escape!" Ivan was led trembling to the Tsar, who glared at him angrily.

"I see from your armor that you are a prince,"
he said. "Why do you come like a thief to steal
my horse?" Ivan bowed his head in shame. Then
the Tsar continued, "I should tell everybody of
your disgrace, but perhaps you can help me."
Ivan looked up hopefully when he heard this.

"In the next kingdom lives a beautiful princess,
the fair Helena," said the Tsar. "I love her
dearly. Bring her to me, and I will pardon you."

Ivan said that he would try, and Tsar Kusman let him go. Ivan hurried to the wolf, and told him what had happened.

Gray Wolf sighed at his foolishness, but forgave him once more. "Get on my back, and let us go to find the fair Helena," he said.

Ivan and the wolf rushed headlong through the night. They went so fast that birds and small animals in the forest were startled as they passed. Then, after many miles, they reached a magnificent palace. "This time *I* will take charge," said Gray Wolf. "This is the home of Tsar Dolmat. Wait for me by this oak tree." And Gray Wolf leaped over the wall and hid in the palace gardens.

After a while, fair Helena came out with her ladies and walked among the flowers. Gray Wolf

sprang out and seized the princess, then sped back to the oak tree. "Hurry!" he shouted. Ivan jumped up behind Helena, and the powerful wolf galloped off. There were angry shouts from the palace, and the sounds of horsemen in pursuit. But Gray Wolf was swifter than the wind, and the three escaped.

Ivan and Helena clung together on Gray Wolf's back. All day he ran powerfully through the forest back toward Tsar Kusman's castle.

Ivan was a handsome youth, and Helena was

beautiful. Before long they had fallen deeply in love, and as they approached the castle Ivan began to look very sad.

Gray Wolf looked over his shoulder and asked what was wrong. Ivan began to weep. "Alas!" he said. "I have to part with Helena, and I cannot. I love her too much, and she loves me."

The wolf slowed down a little, and thought for a while. "Ivan," he said, "I have served you faithfully, but I think there is one more thing I can do for you. I can take the shape of Princess Helena. Leave her here and lead me to the Tsar. When you think of me again I will turn back into a wolf, and return to you."

Ivan was very grateful to his friend, and was amazed to see him change into the exact likeness of Helena. Leaving the real Helena at the edge of the forest, the two made their way to Tsar Kusman.

The Tsar was delighted, and gladly gave the horse with the golden mane to Ivan. Ivan bowed deeply and left. He went back to Helena, and they galloped away on the wonderful horse to get the Firebird.

Meanwhile, Tsar Kusman arranged a marriage. He was to marry fair Helena, but of course she was really far away, with Ivan. The ceremony was about to begin, when Ivan suddenly thought about Gray Wolf—ending the magic spell. As Tsar Kusman was about to kiss his beautiful bride, she turned into a wolf, with a whiskery muzzle and long yellow teeth!

Everybody was so amazed that Gray Wolf was able to slip quietly away. He soon caught up with Ivan and Helena.

There was only one thing left to do: to exchange the horse with the golden mane for the Firebird. But Ivan did not want to lose his beautiful horse. "If you can turn yourself into a princess," he said to Gray Wolf, "surely you could also change into a horse?"

Now you might think that Gray Wolf had already done enough for Ivan. But he was proud of his magic skills, and he was fond of Ivan and Helena. So he turned himself into a horse just like Ivan's splendid steed. "When you think of me again," said the wolf, "I will come back."

Ivan was very pleased. When they neared Tsar Afron's palace, he left Helena with the real horse, and walked on with Gray Wolf, who neighed and tossed his head. Tsar Afron was overjoyed to see the horse with the golden mane,

and he gladly gave the Firebird to Ivan.

Soon Ivan and Helena were galloping, on the real horse, toward Ivan's father's house.

A little while later Ivan thought of Gray Wolf. At that moment Tsar Afron was out hunting on his new horse. He was terrified when it suddenly changed into a snarling wolf and slunk away.

Now Ivan had the Firebird, the wonderful horse, and fair Helena. The wolf, who had caught up with them, padded alongside until they came to the place where he had attacked Ivan's horse. There Gray Wolf stopped. "My work is done," he said. "Now I must leave you." Ivan was very sad to part with his faithful friend.

"Do not say goodbye," said the wolf. "You may have need of me yet." Then he turned, and was soon out of sight in the forest.

Ivan and Helena traveled on toward his home. The journey was long and the weather was hot, and they felt that they must rest. Ivan tied up the horse, and he and Helena lay down on the grass. They were soon fast asleep.

And as they slept, who should come by but Ivan's two brothers. They had been looking for the Firebird, but of course had not been able to find it.

Peter reined his horse and spoke to Vassily. "Look, Ivan has found the Firebird, and see, he has a horse with a golden mane and a beautiful lady, too. This is too much, because Father will give him half the kingdom as well!" Rage filled Peter's heart, and drawing his sword, he killed Ivan. When Helena woke in terror, Vassily pointed his sword at her throat. "You will die too if you say one word to our father about this!"

Poor Helena could do nothing. Vassily put her
on the horse with the golden mane, and the evil
brothers led her to their father's palace.

Ivan lay dead in the forest and ravens circled
over his body. Many days later Gray Wolf came
by and saw his friend surrounded by young birds.
Swiftly he seized one of the fledglings, and the
mother bird flew down and pleaded for its life. "I
will spare your child if you will do something for
me," said Gray Wolf. "Fly over the mountains
and bring me the Water of Life!" The frantic

mother agreed, and flew off. She was soon back with a small vial in her beak.

Quickly Gray Wolf sprinkled the water on Ivan, and slowly the prince woke up. "I have been asleep a long time," he said.

"Get on my back," said Gray Wolf. "We have no time to lose!"

As Ivan, riding on the wolf, drew near to his
father's palace, he saw that banners were flying,
and people in their best clothes were hurrying
toward the gates. Gray Wolf told Ivan what had
happened. "Your brothers found you asleep and
killed you, then they took the Firebird, the horse
with the golden mane, and they stole Helena

away. Today she is to be married to Vassily, and
your brother Peter will have half the kingdom!"

Ivan hurried into the palace. There stood Helena in her wedding dress. When she saw Ivan, she gave a cry of joy. His two brothers were struck dumb with terror.

When the Tsar heard Ivan's story he banished the wicked brothers, and gave half his kingdom to his youngest son instead. Ivan and Helena were married and lived happily ever after.

As for Gray Wolf, perhaps he is still helping people in the endless dark forests of Russia!